HE SAID IT'S OVER... HE LIED!

Deception: He Lied Miniseries

Book 5

Daphne Dennis

TLM Publishing House

Copyright

Social Stamina – 1,2,3 Let's Go!

Titles to help look at things from other perspectives and strengthen your mindset.

The Great Ascension–1,2,3 Let's Go!

Titles to help you gain focus and climb the ladder of success!

How to Start – 1,2,3 Let's Go!

Titles to help you with step-by-step, must-have knowledge of the business world and personal experiences.

Top 10 Questions to Ask Before You…1,2,3 Let's Go!

Titles with must-have questions (and logic behind) for many of life's daily and major decisions.

Find our fiction below!

https://www.ttpublishinghouse.com/legendsreborn

https://www.ttpublishinghouse.com/7wishes

https://www.ttpublishinghouse.com/mallcadet

Social Media

Facebook: tlmpublishinghouse

Website: www.TTpublishinghouse.com

Want to Read for Free?

You may qualify for a spot on our Advance Reader Copy group.

Never heard of an ARC Group?

Simply put, it's a small group of people who are interested in a specific genre and are invited to read books before they're published.

Your feedback can help alter the storyline or even catch an elusive typo!

You're asked to provide an honest review when it is published, and that's it!

You read for free!

Go now to confirm your interest in the ARC Group!
https://www.ttpublishinghouse.com/joinTLMarc

Contents

Drama

Debbie woke up, gasping for air, hair strands sticking on her forehead and her shirt clinging onto her flesh. It was the third time she had woken up to the same nightmare since Matthew died. But, in the dream, instead of him falling, it was her.

"I'm fine. I'm sorry I woke you up." The blonde whispered to Fluffy, her white multi-poo. He was stirring and whining in his sleep, curled up next to her. She began to caress his fur. She glanced at the clock, grimacing at the glaring light that read "03:00" in the dark room. Debbie was too tired to stand up. She didn't want to start her day at 3:00 in the morning, but she was too afraid to fall asleep in case she dreamed of the same thing all over again. So instead, lied in her bed as her thoughts drifted off to her husband, Ed.

Nowadays, she felt like she didn't even know him anymore. It was frustrating to think that she couldn't understand her own husband. Why wasn't he just honest with her? Why was he choosing to keep her in the dark? She was so disheartened by her husband's eccentricities, that she had balled her into a first and had, unknowingly, grabbed a handful of Fluffy's fur. He had made sure she knew though, nudging her with his nose, effectively, as she finally let go.

"Sorry." She said sheepishly. That was the second time she had apologized to Fluffy. He huffed, almost as if he wasn't having it.

"I just... How come I didn't choose some young man... like Randall or Craig when I was younger?" Debbie caught herself asking her dog. "I mean, sure Craig is boring and all that, but he's sensible."

She sighed in annoyance. She wasn't annoyed with anyone but to herself. "What am I even thinking in this ungodly hour… I must be going insane."

The blonde tried the trusted trick of listening to calming sounds to get herself to sleep again. This time, she dreamt of nothing but the void. She didn't mind though. That was better than falling off a building with Matthew smiling maniacally at her. Debbie woke up at around 5:45, drank her cup of coffee before checking the mail. She was in the habit of opening each envelope one by one.

There weren't many bills this time, but there was promotional discount at a local fried chicken store and a grand opening for a laundromat that piqued her interest. Then a familiar name appeared. She picked the letter up with disbelief and curiosity before ripping the overly scented envelope open. Inside was the most obnoxious color of brown with white florals and letters with a bigger gold font that said ***"Craig & Jillian"***.

… Who the heck was Jillian?

Debbie skimmed through the barely readable invitation, gasping softly to herself once she realized it was an engagement invitation, and that Craig was marrying someone named Jillian. He couldn't have known her very long. For a moment, it felt like a slap in the face for the blonde. She was just thinking about how she could've just chosen someone like Craig and, lo-and-behold, he's engaged.

Even after she arrived at work at the winery, her mind was still all over the place. *Craig, bald, boring Craig, found a girl who's willing to put up with his ego. Now there's the surprise of the century.*

"Hey Debbie! Are you good?" Patty elbowed her softly as they walked towards the vineyard to pick some grapes. Debbie shook her head, looking at her with cynicism in as she spoke.

"Craig's getting married."

"Craig? Wait... you mean bald, boring Craig? **THE** Craig that kept on following you?"

"I know, right? Unbelievable."

"How did you know?"

Debbie scoffed. "He sent me an invitation for their engagement party for the day after tomorrow."

"He did?!"

The blonde only nodded before the other asked again, "So, are you going?"

That made Debbie stop dead in her tracks. Is she going? Now, that's a good question. She tried recalling the information written on the letter, frowning before clicking her tongue.

"I'm not familiar with the location."

"What do you mean?" Patty asked, confused.

"He bought a new house. Probably for him and his future wife to settle in."

"Oh... wow."

An awkward silence fell between them. Debbie wondered if Patty was thinking the same thing she was. *That could have been my house.*

And, truthfully, it could've been. If Debbie had only gone ahead and done what her mother was pushing her to do, she could've been inviting people to her engagement party at that house, once she had divorced Ed, of course. Oddly, it felt strange thinking about it. The thought of living a life with Craig was off putting, but, at the same time, she wondered if maybe she could've learned and adapted to him as time went on.

"So… Are you going or… Not that I'm forcing you or anything. Just… you know, aren't you curious about what kind of girl he's marrying? To be honest, I am curious." Patty nodded, as if agreeing to herself, as she pluck grapes and delicately placed them inside her woven basket. She wasn't wrong. Debbie was intrigued. What type of girl was this Jillian that Craig was in such a hurry to marry her?

***

Debbie did end up going to the party, and her desire to meet Craig's fiancé was realized. Unfortunately for Debbie, Jillian was a talker. And, she met Debbie, she latched onto her and wouldn't stop talking. She talked her ear off about how she'd gotten there, what a long story it was.

Debbie had gone to the party because she thought it might be the last time, she saw Craig. She went just to satiate her curiosity. She wasn't prepared for at all for how nice Craig's house was. The house seemed to speak to her. She could see herself living in it. It was a two-story house with a beautiful brown, shingle roof, Dover white walls, and a much lighter color of beige in the garage, which could park four cars. The front door was made of rosewood and was a double door.

Debbie marveled at the glass wall next to the front door. All the windows were like two-way mirrors. So people could see inside but not outside. Of course, the greatest thing about the house was the vast yard with green trees and bushes everywhere. It had clean cut grass and vibrant flowers planted beautifully, looking like a mini maze. And, if she thought the outside was beautiful, she was unprepared for how glorious the inside was.

Goodness. This house is breathtaking. Debbie knocked on the door, and someone opened it. "Oh! You must be Debbie! Come in, Come in!" A loud and obnoxious woman who looked like she had 1 pound of make-up on rushed to her side with a huge grin. From then on, she chatted with her like they'd been good friends since birth.

Debbie found herself stuck in a conversation she didn't want to be in. It was little awkward, hearing the woman talk about her like she had known her for years. Debbie could hardly get a word in edgewise.

"Craig must've said good things about me." The blonde chuckled in feigned innocence while the woman only nodded, waving her hand, unprovoked, in the air almost intentionally just to show off her neon marbled stiletto nails. The blonde didn't usually like to point out people's faults. But she found Jillian to be obnoxious. She believed that confidence is key when it came to outfits, but Jillian's outfit was so over the top that it made Debbie scoff inwardly.

First was her bleached blonde hair... It was so huge that an eagle could use it as a nest for its entire family. It was three times bigger than her face. Not only that, but she had a little tiara on top of her head. Debbie was sure that blonde wasn't really her natural color because she could see black roots peeking through. It was too obvious not to notice. Secondly, her makeup looked weird. It looked as if she was wearing a thick mask painted with bright glittery green on the inner eyelids that faded into a smokey seaweed color. Her fake lashes were too thick. Debbie wondered how she could still keep her eyes open with them on, yet her eyebrows were close to non-existent.

Her eyelids must be so heavy. The blonde inwardly commented while Jillian kept on blabbering. The next thing Debbie noted was her green semi-formal dress that stopped mid-thigh, sleeves reaching up to her elbows with white leafy patterns and baggy pockets. She was quite sure that she had seen a similar pattern for a table cloth at the local department store but didn't dare to point it out. It physically pained her how Jillian paired the dress with brown velvet ankle boots. It definitely didn't match.

Debbie had always been a bit of a fashionista so she knew a thing or two what matched and what didn't. Debbie was clad in a floral periwinkle-colored round neckline dress with see-through sleeves that she paired with pointed white flat shoes. If people didn't know any better, they would've mistaken Debbie as the bride-to-be instead of Jillian. The theme for the party was florals, as specified in the invitation so the guests wore anything floral, from dresses to Hawaiian shirts.

Craig was sporting a Hawaiian shirt himself as he made his way towards the two ladies. Debbie fought the urge to retch as she bore witness to how Craig snaked his arm around Jillian's waist as the woman snorted in a way that made Debbie's skin crawl in second-hand embarrassment.

"You two seem to be having a good time talking." Craig commented as Jillian batted her fake lashes at him like a doll. They snuggled close to each other like two peas in a pod.

"I was telling her about how I was planning to do the interior and the yard over to add more colors to our house. Maybe some golds too just to make it extra pretty." Jillian said, doe-eyed, as the man looked at her. "I also want a backyard pool for the vacant lot."

"Wow. That's a lot of work to do and probably expensive, too. I suppose the wedding's all set then?" Debbie spoke before she could stop herself. *That darn tongue of mine.*

The bride-to-be only grinned at her almost as if she'd proud of how much money she was about to spend while patting Craig's chest softly. "Craig has got all the money for the work, right babe?"

"Of course, love. Anything to make my queen happy." The man replied before being called away by one of his friends. After Craig left, Jillian leaned close to Debbie and whispered, "You know, I was deciding between two men, John and Craig, but I chose Craig because he had a bigger house and can support my lavish lifestyle."

Debbie could only blink back at her, stunned that this woman blatantly admitted that she was only marrying Craig to live her "trophy wife" fantasy.

"Do you love him?" The blonde asked, feeling sorry for the man for the first time.

The other woman giggled, patting Debbie's shoulder before winking. She said, "Oh, Debbie. Love can only go so far when you have an empty bank account and a grumbling stomach."

After that, the woman left to entertain the other guests. The blonde didn't feel well and had to quietly slip outside, feeling shocked by Jillian's last statement. She was worried about Craig. Although it was true, she had felt indifferent before, after what she had just heard, she couldn't stomach not doing or saying anything to the man. So, she tried searching for him until she found him descending from the second floor. Quick on her feet, she immediately walked towards him, surprising the man whom she seemed willing to have a conversation with after all these years, trying to distance herself.

"Can I talk to you for a minute?" Debbie asked, quiet, but determined. Craig, in his confusion, only nodded and ushered Debbie to the garden where they could be alone.

"So, what's up?" Craig asked, hands in pockets with a quirked eyebrow.

"Oh… I just wanted to… you know, congratulate you for the engagement and all that." Debbie inwardly scolded herself for not being straightforward. *Why can I never just be direct?* The man genuinely smiled at her, and that made her pity him more.

Craig said, "Thanks. I'm thrilled now that I've met Jillian."

"How did you two meet, anyway? I'd never heard about her until I read the letter."

"We met each other on a business trip. We hung out, and she told me she chose me over a man named John because I made her feel loved."

No, she chose you because you had more money. Debbie thought, but held her tongue.

"That's sweet... How long were you dating before the engagement?"

The man thought for a while. "Maybe a month?"

"A mo- You really wanted to tie the knot. You only dated for a month? Isn't that too impulsive?" She questioned, unable to believe how hasty Craig was when it came to decision-making. Craig only knitted his eyebrows and glared at her, not seeming to like that Debbie was judging his love life.

"I know it may sound weird, but I feel like we're connected. She's, my soulmate."

"A soulmate you just met *a month* ago. Craig, I know I don't do this often, but don't you think you should really think this through? Marriage is not something you can back out of even if you were to divorce. It's not something you can erase. Even if you divorce, you'll never be single again in legal documents."

"You think I don't know that? Look, I don't know why you're trying to talk me out of this marriage, but I'm going to marry Jillian, and no one's stopping me."

Debbie frowned at him. "I didn't mean it like that, Craig. Sure, we had our misunderstanding but believe me when I say I am concerned for you with this marriage."

The man looked at her, staring intently before sighing. "You know, Debbie. If you only said these words to me two weeks ago, then I would've probably never proposed to her at all."

Debbie grew confused when Craig smiled at her, a pained, sad smile she never thought he'd give her.

Craig continued, "I'm not supposed to tell anyone this, but I've been eyeing this house for almost a year now. It caught my attention because it reminded me of you. I thought to myself that maybe, if you were to ever accept me, we could build our own family here. You could have every space you want to decorate, repaint the walls to your heart's content and redo the interior all over again."

"Craig…"

"I know." He laughed, sadly. "It's what I had in mind when I saw it. But then those visions will remain just visions now. I waited, Debbie. Heaven knows how long I've waited. I knew that you were in a rocky relationship and separated. But I waited for you to give me some kind of indication that you might like me, even a little. But you never gave me the chance. You never looked my way unlike Jillian."

"I'm sorry…"

"Don't be. You don't need to be sorry. I'm happy, Debbie. I have more than enough money to keep her satisfied and happy. I have the prenup and everything ready so don't worry about it. And whatever happens here on after, I'll stick to my decision."

Wow… so this was the side of Craig I never saw. I only saw his awkwardness and eccentricity.

"I'm happy for you then." She smiled as the air between them finally cleared. The two had a great time talking unlike before. It felt as if they'd come to a mutual understanding as Craig bombarded her with fun facts, and she laughed playfully at how useless those facts were for daily life. It was clear to her that the man was elated. He was glowing and looking more relaxed.

That was until her mother butted in the conversation after finding the two of them talking.

"This could have been you, Deborah, if only you'd listened to me. You two could've been the perfect couple." Her mother berated her with a disappointed head shake.

"Mom, please. Show some respect to Craig and his future wife."

"You could have been the future wife instead of that obnoxious woman. How can you ever let such a man go and be married to a bum?"

Debbie clenched her fist, trying not to lose her temper. Craig seemed to notice her rage. Not wanting to make anything worse, the groom-to-be excused himself from the conversation. The blonde was thankful for that. She didn't want to ruin his party even though she didn't like his fiancée.

"How can you call Jillian obnoxious in front of Craig, mom? Have you lost it?" She hissed, frustrated that her mother only ever brought her embarrassment and shame.

The older woman scoffed, rolling her eyes and crossing her arms. "What I was saying was true. Craig must know that by now. That Jillian girl took your place because you're too slow to act."

"I am not slow to act. I do not want to act on anything because I never wanted to marry Craig. Sure, now that we're on good terms, I would've reconsidered. But he's boring, mom. I don't want to be a trophy wife. I want a life of my own."

"That's the problem with you, Deborah. You live too much in the moment without a thought for your future. That's exactly why you ended up in this situation. Married to a worthless man."

Her mother gave her a taunting look, raising an eyebrow before looking at her from top to bottom and back up again. "Maybe you're right. You and Ed are meant to be together because now, you're both struggling to make ends meet instead of living off Craig's good fortune. If you only inherited a single trait from me, you would've made the right decision. I'm so disappoint to call a dimwit my daughter."

Debbie could barely remember what happened next. She was so emotionally traumatized by her mother's words to even utter a word, let alone figure out what to do next. The blonde knew that her mother was always strict with her, always on her back about everything and was always a control freak. But she had never heard her say those words out loud before in the public where someone could've heard. She had done it in someone else's house, which humiliated Debbie even more and made her realize that her mom didn't value her at all. What she could remember, however, was someone pulling her into a hug, warmth against the coldness of her own mother's words as her vision was greeted with black. A solid figure had embraced her, that much she knew, and that solid figure felt familiar.

"Just because you're her mother doesn't mean you get to treat her however you want to. You might have given birth to her, but you were never a mother."

The voice made Debbie feel something inside her surge, agony, anger, loneliness. His words cut so deep it felt like the life was being drained out of her. Instinctively, she clung onto his shirt, burying her head deeper in his chest while the man tightened his hold around her.

"You don't have a say in this matter, Ed." Her mother replied to the man. "You ruined everything I had planned for her."

"Planned for her? Really? Or things you had planned for yourself?"

"How dare you-"

"No. How dare you treat your own blood like that. You don't deserve to be called a mother."

"And you don't deserve to be called her husband!" Debbie's mother shrieked so loud it might've attracted some attention. Debbie hoped not. This much drama was enough for a whole year.

"I know. And I don't deny that. I may not be the best husband to Debbie. But I see her for who she is. Her passion, her dedication to the things she loved to do. The little things you find as faults, I find worthy of praise. All she ever wanted was a life of her own, but you never liked that idea because it doesn't benefit you. You never wanted her to be happy or else you wouldn't have hurt her this much."

"I NEVER LAID A HAND ON HER!"

"***Which is worse***. Do you know how much pain and trauma you've put Debbie through with your words? The words you say and then forget the next second just because you think it's justifiable for a parent to demean their own child? You never loved your daughter. All you were doing was trying to make her have the life you wanted to live."

"Ed..." Debbie finally spoke, crying silently in his arms. "Let's go. Please."

Ed nodded with a hushed voiced, giving her stunned mother one last disapproving look before ushering the crying woman to her car, taking the driver's seat before leaving the place. They drove off in silence as Debbie sobbed. The blonde froze when she felt his hand gently grab hers. The man stayed focus on the road but still gave her a sign that he was paying attention to her.

"Do you want to head straight home?" He quietly asked, glancing at her once before looking back straight ahead.

"No." The woman replied, sinking into her seat, her eyes and nose red and puffy. "I don't want to be alone right now."

That was all it took for Ed to realize what a burden his wife was probably carrying. Debbie could guess that as his eyes, though not looking at her, turned solemn, while he pursed his lips. He drove down the long, quiet road, passing by familiar bits of scenery, until Ed stopped the car. The woman felt nostalgia hitting her as she exited the car, street lamps already on as the sky got darker. She knew she told him she didn't want to go home just yet, but she never expected for him to drive them here.

Memory Lane

"It's changed a little bit, hasn't it?" Debbie looked over her shoulder as Ed locked the car. She smiled tenderly, nodding, as she took in her surroundings. The changes were small indeed, the small stalls where they used to buy cotton candy weren't there anymore, the trees around the park were definitely fewer in some areas, but the ambience was still there. It brought back so many memories.

"Remember when we used to sneak here because your mother never let you go out with me?" Ed chuckled, standing beside Debbie who softly hummed.

Debbie said, "I remember it like it happened yesterday."

"Do you think that bench is still there?" The man asked.

"I'm not sure. I can't see it from here."

"Want to look for it, then?"

The blonde looked at him, letting out a delicate laugh at his amused face.

"Sure."

They started walking around the park, pointing out the things they remember being a part of their love story. The spots they used to frequent on secret dates, and the little things they used to talk about and dream about. She noted the now drained fountain where they used to toss coins in the belief that it would grant their wishes. He pointed out the old Banyan tree they would rest at while talking about their hopes for the future. Debbie could feel herself growing a lot calmer as they continued walking down the familiar path.

"Whoa. It's still intact. I guess they kept it for sentimental value." Ed mused. Indeed, they must have done that. It wasn't nearly as nice as the new benches and tables, the grass around the old wooden bench was a bit more overgrown as trees stood where they hadn't before. Debbie watched as the man started slowly circling around the bench, eyes a little squinted as the flashlight on his phone became the only source of light for his apparent search for something.

"What are you doing?" She asked, nearly laughing at how ridiculous he looked while searching. "Shh. I'm trying to look for- oh! Come here. Quick!" Ed beamed at her as he hurriedly waved his hand for her to come closer. Debbie did despite her confusion, she herself squinting at the spot where Ed's flashlight was pointing.

"Do you see it?" He whispered, so close that she could feel his breath. The blonde shuddered, perhaps due to the cold night or something else entirely. She wasn't sure. Her eyes widened when she finally realized what he was trying to point out, emotions overflowing as she turned her head towards him.

"How long ago did you do this?" She whispered, lips quivering. Ed sadly smiled, averting his gaze.

Ed replied, "After our first date."

Debbie let out a shuddered breath, blinking in an attempt to stop the tears from falling. She couldn't believe how long it went unnoticed to her, those little engraved initials of them both. For many, this would be foolish and childish, but to her, she realized it was Ed's confession. *He initialed our names?* It was a very romantic thing for a man to do who was never romantic.

It must have been the surroundings and atmosphere that pushed Debbie to lean in and steal a kiss. The blonde was the first to pull away, blushing madly like she had just experienced her first kiss.

"Want an Icy Freeze?" The man spoke after a long period of silence, making Debbie smile from ear to ear.

She felt like they were reliving moments from years ago. *We got a slushie on our first date.*

"I'd love one, yes."

Thankfully, the convenience store they went to back in the day was still operating, although the store had a different owner now. Still, the store had kept its products in its usual places. It was as if they had stepped into a time machine back to the past. As they entered, Debbie heard the little ring of the store bell. She smiled to herself as she remembered hearing the same exact sound almost every day at one point in her life. They walked past the candy section, turning right to where the chips and packed cookies were before finally arriving at the slushie machine. Aside from the machine, everything was kept in its original state, the woman noted internally as Ed grabbed two large cups on the side.

"This is probably a new machine. It's been years after all." Ed spoke as if answering her inner question as she just nodded absentmindedly. Though she wouldn't lie and say she didn't feel something odd as she looked at the round mirror at the upper corner near the machine, feeling that someone was watching them.

It was probably just the cashier making sure we're not stealing anything.

Yet it didn't feel like that somehow. It felt like that person was waiting for something to happen... Something regarding them using the machine.

"Take cover!" Debbie heard Ed scream as he pulled her to hide behind one of the aisle dividers. She shrieked when something loud and bright shook the products off their shelves, and the store's sprinklers activated.

"What's happening?!" she screamed over the loud alarm of the store as Ed pulled her out and back to her car.

"Someone's after us. Put your seatbelt on." Ed simply replied, focusing on getting the engine starting. Debbie hurriedly, and clumsily, put the seatbelt on, clutching the piece of polyester fiber in fear as her eyes trembled.

Someone was after them? Of course. It didn't matter where or when or how, those people wanted them dead. Ed drove off, a little past the speeding limit, and had Debbie, who admittedly was never a very religious woman, praying vehemently that they wouldn't crash and burn.

"We need to stick together. Who knows what tricks they still have up their sleeves? It's better for us to stay together at this point than to be alone. At least until this issue is resolved." The man suggested, looking over at his wife who was pale and looking like she was ready to vomit. They reached Debbie's house in no time thanks to how fast Ed drove, although the blonde would never want to experience that ever again. His words only sunk in when the man locked the house instead of leaving.

"Are you staying over?" She asked, oblivious.

"I told you earlier-" he sighed, running a hand over his hair. "Whatever. Just stick with me, and don't go anywhere without your phone. It's hard enough that you keep going places. My motel room must be bugged. They must have overheard me saying to myself that I was going to get you a slushie."

"So, you're going to stay over." Debbie wasn't entirely sure what she wanted him to say. Maybe she was waiting for him to admit that he wanted to go back to being "husband and wife" or that he would return home, but that never happened.

"Only until this mess is over..." the blonde couldn't hear the rest of it as he mumbled the words. She bit her lips, furrowing her eyebrows at him in frustration before finally blurting out, "I still love you."

Confession

Ed looked stunned, as she expected honestly, but that did nothing to deter her emotions as she continued.

Debbie said, "I still love you. And I realized that after what happened earlier. That kiss, that place, it brought back the feelings I've been trying to suppress."

"You're just tired-"

"I'm not. I'm not delirious or overwhelmed with emotions or being too oversentimental just because we reminisced about the past. Ed, I still love you. And I don't want to deny that anymore."

The blonde waited. And she waited. She didn't know whether she was going to experience rejection or otherwise. She continued to wait for him to answer. But he never replied. Instead, he turned his eyes away from her. It infuriated her. She felt like he was messing with her emotions. *How sadistic do you have to be to do this?* Debbie tried to sleep that night knowing full well that her husband was in the living room. So close yet so far. She laughed ironically at how much they'd been going down memory lane. This had happened before too, back when their relationship started getting confusing. It was those times that she thought they were just having their usual conflicts, but, no, that was the beginning of when they became estranged. She felt then the way she felt now... abandoned.

In the morning, Ed was no longer in the living room. Had the whole thing been a dream? Debbie forced herself not to think about it too much since she knew it would only confuse her head and heart more. She got ready and headed to work, too tired and pre-occupied to notice someone tailing her from afar. The blonde had an interesting conversation with Patty at work. It distracted her enough that she was able to stop dwelling on how frustrated she was with her husband.

Patty showed off her new necklace while on a break. Debbie, of course, then had to ask where she got it and that's how the conversation started.

"I got it from Randy." She spoke with a blush on her cheeks, fiddling with the shiny metal around her neck. Randy was the guy she'd been seeing according to her stories, although Patty had never introduced Randall to Debbie, which Debbie found odd. If she was seeing someone, she would want Patty to meet him.

"So, when can I meet this 'Randy' you keep talking about?" Debbie teased, but Patty's smile only turned into a frown.

"Oh, but you already know him."

"I do?"

Patty giggled. "Of course! You've known him even longer than I have."

Longer than... **Oh**.

"Randy... Randall?"

Debbie gasped when the other nodded shyly.

"Oh, my god, since when?!"

"Remember when he punched Ed at your mom's party? He slipped his number in my purse that night because he thought I was cute. We went on a few dates, and now we're seeing each other."

"Really?! I'm so happy for you, Patty!" The blonde hugged her friend who returned the kind gesture.

"Thanks. I really like him, you know. He's such a gentleman." The brunette sighed like a love-sick woman.

Debbie nudged her as she playfully wiggled her eyebrow. "You really did meet your prince charming, huh?"

They chattered a while longer until it was time to work again. By the end of the shift, Patty asked her if she wanted to have some drinks to celebrate her love life, but the blonde declined. She needed to go to the hardware store to buy a door bolt. When asked why, she simply said that she wanted extra safety after what happened before. Patty didn't insist for her to come, saying she understood her point of view and asking for her to be careful. They hugged once more before parting ways.

The hardware store was opposite the road to her home so she knew if she didn't rush, she'd probably get stuck in traffic. She quickly made her way inside the store, asking a clerk to point out where the door bolts were as she sped walked to them. What she didn't expect was to find Trish in line after finding the right bolt. They exchanged greetings until Trish opened up about how she was feeling guilty because she kept thinking that it was her fault that Judy died.

"Why do you say that?" The blonde asked, concerned.

"I tend to gossip a lot. And maybe that's why someone heard about her and killed her. I don't know, I just feel like I shouldn't have said anything about her. And Herman too." Trish whispered, gripping the rolls of wallpaper in her arms.

"Hey, it's not your fault. Never think that it's your fault." She paused, wondering if her words could give her assurance before continuing. "Judy was involved with some things. It was just a terrible thing, but you had nothing to do with it so you shouldn't feel responsible for it. Trust me."

They parted ways, and Trish gave her a thankful smile before Debbie drove home. She was lucky enough to dodge the traffic, coming home to no one but her dog.

"What was I expecting, really…" she mumbled, changing into a more comfortable outfit before deciding to install the door bolt herself. It wasn't easy, but at least there were some instructions to follow. Once she had successfully done so, she made her way to the kitchen to find a takeout box from Kentucky Fried Chicken. On top, was a small letter with familiar handwriting.

Don't skip your meals. The vexed expression she sported on her face showed that she knew exactly who left it there.

"Jerk. How can you be so frustrating to understand?" She asked to no one as she opened the takeout box. She sat there, munching on the delicious chicken while thinking about her life and all her mistakes. It seemed that love was in the air with everyone around her. They were all falling in love and finding love, yet she and her husband were still estranged. Debbie reminisced about the first time she met Ed, how it wasn't about money or anything else like that with them. They were young, and she felt like she could be herself the most when around him. She felt so comfortable, like she could be who she wanted to be with him.

He was funny and eccentric in a good way. There was never a dull moment when they talked. They understood and knew each other, at least that's how it felt before things fell apart. Now, she was starting to feel like she had messed up her life, and that there was no way for her to be happy again.

***

Debbie received the news from the police that Bobo, the homeless man, was released from police custody the next day as they did have not enough evidence to detain him any longer. The blonde felt guilty that she put the poor man in a cell because of being strange. She wanted to apologize but was afraid that Bobo would no longer want to see her, especially since Matthew had ended up being the bad guy and not him. Yet she had believed that Bobo was a bad guy just because he was dirty, poor, and a little cooky. What a huge mistake.

Debbie heard the doorbell ring and opened it, only to find Ed standing there. She looked directly into Ed's eyes as he stood there, clutching a single sunflower he had probably uprooted at someone's unsuspecting yard illegally. He asked her out on a date after disappearing without a word.

"Give me half an hour to prepare at least."

She was still mad at him though for not telling her everything. But she would lie if she said she wasn't curious about what he had to say.

It wasn't as extravagant of a date as before, not nearly as expensive as the lunch she had with Craig, nor as scenic as Matthew's date. But she'd always dreamt of having dates with him no matter how simple they were. She didn't care.

They arrived at the local diner, one that she always passed by while on her way to work. It was minimalist, woods and greens as a theme with fairy lights around the ceiling. The music was relatively mellow and jazzy. Ed looked through the menu. Debbie could hardly focus on the menu so she decided to get whatever Ed ordered, ending up with a mushroom soup for an appetizer and a mini seafood platter for the main course. Ed did ask her if she wanted anything more like dessert or side dish but she declined. Admittedly, she just wanted to know what he was thinking by asking her out on a date.

"You must be wondering, huh?" The blonde glanced at him as she, unheeding, twirled her fork around the plate.

She sighed, dropping the fork gently before leaning backwards with a frown. "I just don't get you, Ed. You were gone the next morning after I told you I still love you, and then you entered my house to give me takeout and now this? I'm not a mind-reader, and I'm so frustrated right now I could punch you if we weren't in public."

"Sorry. I understand that you're confused and, believe me, I know how frustrated you must have been."

"Then why do you still frustrate me? If you know how stressful this is to me then why do you still do it?"

"Because I was afraid. I got so scared that I wouldn't be able to protect you and that I'd just hear news about finding your body on TV." He gulped, genuine fear in his voice as he lowered his gaze. "You've always been the smart one, and that's proven with how you're doing an incredible job with this case on your own. But that's what I fear. That you're always one step ahead of me the whole time. That I'm falling behind instead of solving this case for you."

"Why are you so attached to this case in the first place?" She paused, negative thoughts clouding her better judgement. "Were you seeing Judy behind my back? Is that it?"

The offended look Ed gave her made her want to take back those last words. However, no one could blame her for thinking that, especially when Ed refused to tell her anything at all.

The man replied. "I would never cheat on you. I can't even imagine cheating on you."

"Then why didn't you just tell me that? And why don't you just tell me what's really going on? Say it straight to my face. I'm sick of guessing every single thought that runs to your head."

They both sat silently, the soft chattering and low jazz music entering their ears.

"I'm interested in this case because I feel responsible for her murder."

"Not you too. Why does everyone think they're at fault for her death?" She mumbled to herself.

"What was that?"

"I said why do you think it's your fault?"

Ed hesitantly looked around, leaning closer with a low whisper. "Because I don't think Judy was a drug addict, nor do I think that Philip is a drug dealer."

"What?" Now things were taking a different turn.

The man continued. "I think she's been leaking government secrets."

Debbie would've laughed at his statement if not for how serious he was. Because, God, that sounded ludicrous. Judy, **that Judy**, was leaking government secrets? That was worse than Bobo telling her about the people on the trees.

"Are you sure you're not... hallucinating? Are you sure that sachet I saw in your room wasn't drugs?"

"I'm not. My head is clear, and I'm sure because I borrowed money from Philip after Judy recommended him to me."

"Why would you want to borrow money? You could've just asked me, and we could've discussed this together."

"Because it was for you." Ed said, looking up to her, emotions raw and bare. "Because I wanted to help you build your own dream business. I felt bad all those years that you put us, me and our children, first. You barely had time for yourself. You basically raised those kids on your own because I was always gone. I tried to provide, to save in order to give you that, but it wasn't enough. That's why I approached Judy since she had real estate and business knowledge. I asked for advice. She directed me to Philip, and that's how I got involved with this mess."

All this time she misunderstood him. He was doing his best to give Debbie her dream... She felt sick to her stomach. It was her own paranoid thoughts that had kept them apart. She should have trusted him.

"You did that for me... Yet I doubted and pushed you away..." she whispered, her vision clouding. Debbie fought back tears when Ed reached out to hold her hand, giving it a reassuring squeeze.

Ed said, "It wasn't your fault. You had every right to doubt me. I should've been more careful. I... I just wanted to surprise you. I never meant to put you in this mess."

"I'm scared, Ed," the blonde revealed with quivering lips. "I'm worried that I'm going to be killed next. I can't bear the thought of our children losing me, losing us."

"I won't let that happen," he promised. "I won't let anything happen to you."

They continued their conversation at home, making a detour to buy some canned beers to share. Ed, still sober, told her everything willingly this time. How he didn't know that Philip was a spy when he asked for a loan to help her start a business. How he got so terrified when those men in suits started threatening him and asking him where the "papers" were. Debbie could remember the time he left home. She thought he was just done with their marriage and wanted nothing more of it when the truth was that he was keeping his family safe by moving away.

She leaned in and rested her head on his shoulder. Ed didn't move away. He was presumably too tipsy and too invested with his story to notice.

He continued on by telling her how his trip to Judy's cabin had gone. He wanted to ask her about it when he looked around her cabin and realized she had information from the nuclear lab which she was selling to the North Koreans.

"You mean like lasers and chemical warfare?" Debbie asked, wide eyed.

"Yes… How did you know about those things?"

"I saw Herman's room. It had those things as well. Bobo also talked about them."

"Bobo?"

"The homeless man that was lurking around Judy's cabin."

"Wait, hold on. Did you just say you were in Herman's room?" Ed eyed her with suspicion but Debbie just rolled her eyes.

Debbie explained. "It's not what you think. I went there because I was snooping around. I thought Herman was the murderer so I tried looking for clues and stumbled into that specific room. It was filled with papers related to nuclear and chemical warfare. It was crazy."

***

If only I could find those papers. That would be the key to solving this whole mess. Debbie and Ed stood in her bedroom where Fluffy was jolted awake, running away to sleep somewhere else comfortably. Debbie grabbed her laptop, almost falling down the stairs before reaching Ed who looked at her weirdly. She opened a specific folder before giving it to the man.

"What's this?" he asked, clearly not following whatever she had uncovered.

"It's a letter given to me by Judy."

That made Ed more serious, gazing at the glowing screen in silence. Debbie bit her lips, anxious. "Do you think you can solve it? I tried, but I don't get it at all."

"I think... I can... Just... Give me a minute... If this is what I think it is... Huh... Oh!" he exclaimed, typing furiously on her laptop as the screen loaded to a bank website in Switzerland. Debbie witnessed how Ed scrolled and scrolled until he stopped, highlighting a specific set of words and pasting them into a new note where he began typing too. The blonde's jaw dropped at what she saw when he finished typing.

"You cracked the code." She spoke, awed by her husband who amazingly decoded Judy's message for her. It

was a bank account number where the papers — or nuclear secrets — were most definitely secured.

"Judy was trying to keep the secret away. She wasn't selling them to the North Koreans. She was trying to keep it from them." Ed announced before looking at his awestruck wife. "Let's give the information to the authorities in the lab. I'm sure they'll know what to do with it."

He then gave Debbie a soft smile, relief overflowing from his reaction. *"We found it. The papers. You're going to be safe now."*

The man was surprised when Debbie leaped into his arms. Lucky for them both, Ed had quick reflexes. He successfully kept both the laptop and Debbie from falling to the ground.

"That was reckless, Debbi-"

He was rendered speechless as the blonde took it upon herself to silence him with her lips. Dumbfounded, he stared at her as she pulled away.

"I love you." She told him, voice unwavering and certain.

Debbie was over the moon when Ed kissed her back, passionately, as he let the laptop finally fall to the ground when he picked up the blonde. It was messy, and steamy, and Debbie love every second of it. She giggled softly at how Ed rushed to remove his shirt while straddling her on the bed. She hadn't seen him this impatient since their honeymoon, and it was endearing. She pulled him down for a kiss, softer and quicker.

"I love you, Ed," she repeated, loving how she could freely tell him that again. And she loved it more how the man smiled back with the gentlest of kisses in between saying, "I love you too."

Debbie was happy, absolutely elated now that they were almost done with the case. They just needed to get Philip arrested for working for the North Koreans as a double agent, and then everything would be over. They spent the night together making love. And in the heat of the moment, a question was asked.

"Will you marry me again, Debbie?"

The woman choked a sob, smiling dearly as she held his face. **"I will."**

The Lie

Debbie woke up the next day with the sound of a faint clinking coming from downstairs. She mumbled incoherently as her eyebrows knit together, and her lips formed into a frown. She then patted the spot beside her, her frown deepening when she realized the warmth next to her was gone. The blonde was certain that she fell asleep with someone beside her. Last night's activity was too vivid not to be real.

"Ed?" the blonde groggily asked, raising her head slightly to see that there was indeed no one on the spot where the man was supposed to be. Puzzled and a little worried, Debbie went downstairs clad in her nightgown as she followed the gradually increasing noise from the kitchen.

"Ed?" she asked again, cautiously peeking and was honestly surprised to see the man preparing some homemade breakfast. It smelled like burnt pancakes. Debbie rummaged through her mind to try to think of a time when Ed had fixed something for her but couldn't think of one, so her bewildered expression was not for no reason. Upon hearing her, Ed looked up, smiling shyly at her while finishing up by pouring a glass of fresh milk into two glasses.

"You're awake. Was I too noisy?" He gently asked while walking towards her and putting his arms around her waist. If someone told Debbie that she'd finally feel and see Ed's affection in a way that was easy-to-understand days prior to this moment, she would've looked at them like they'd grown two heads and snakes for hair. But this was that moment, the awaited moment wherein Ed would make her feel loved wholeheartedly.

The blonde hummed in satisfaction, eyes closed as she felt his lips on her forehead followed by the softest whisper of, "Good morning."

"Hm... Morning," she happily replied with a lazy yet bright smile. Ed chuckled at how adorable she looked, leading her towards the table before pulling out a chair for her.

"Look at you. I might get used to this if you keep this up." Debbie teased, giggling while Ed sat in front of her with a satisfied smile.

"Go ahead. I plan to treat you better from now on."

That caused butterflies to erupt in her stomach, fluttering all over the place as she could feel warmth rushing to her face. Lord, if this was a dream, then Debbie would gladly stay asleep forever. But it wasn't — this was no longer a far-fetched fantasy but a blooming reality, and that thought made her heart grew warmer.

"So... how is it on a scale of 1 to 10?" the man asked, seemingly reluctant and visibly nervous when Debbie took a big bite. The blonde, feeling playful, munched more while furrowing her eyebrows.

"I think... 3?" she replied, trying her best not to break into a fit of laughter at his defeated look before speaking again. "I'm just kidding. I think it's great. A little burnt, but still great nonetheless."

The blonde then smiled, endeared at the relief that flooded his eyes. She spoke, "Thank you for making breakfast even though you didn't have to. Did you wake up early just to make these?"

"I'm used to waking up early anyway, so I took the chance to freshen up and cooked you some breakfast after. It's not much. But I wanted to make up for the years I've pushed you and our children aside unknowingly." His voice then became a lot more serious. "I promise to be better, Debbie. To you and to our family."

The two enjoyed their breakfast, talking about their plans for after they closed the case, both agreeing that a family trip to Santorini sounded amazing. Debbie volunteered to wash the dishes in order for Ed to email the information on Judy's card to the lab to quicken the pace of closing the murder case.

"Hey, Ed. I'm thinking of going out for a while." The blonde said as soon as she entered the living room, sporting a new set of clothes, as she had taken a bath after she finished washing the dishes. Ed was typing on her laptop. The man looked up, the typing sound going silent.

Ed asked, "Where to?"

"I'm going to see Bobo to apologize for falsely accusing him and to say that we've cracked the case. I'm worried about him. He's homeless, and I think he needs help. It won't take long, though."

"I'm going with you." the man responded, glancing back to the screen as the typing sound echoed once more, faster than before.

"But you're still-"

With a loud click from the keyboard, Ed set aside the laptop. He stood up, grabbing his jacket and taking the car keys from Debbie who was taken aback.

"Done. Let's go."

"You don't have to go with me. I'll be fine."

"I know you're responsible, Debbie. But I'll die of worry if I stay here so I'm coming with you."

She was still getting used to this side of Ed. The blonde followed without a word. She locked the door, thankful that Fluffy was still deep in slumber inside before entering the car on the passenger side. Ed had insisted on driving, so she let him. Going down the familiar road, Debbie suddenly felt a jolt of chills, looking out her car window to check if someone was following them. There was no one. Even the suited man that used to park near her house was gone. Placing a hand in front of her chest, she could clearly feel the pounding of her heart, her gut warning her of something she couldn't quite pinpoint.

"Is everything okay?" She heard her husband asked, seeming to notice her uneasiness.

"I don't... I just suddenly felt chills," was her honest reply. That feeling didn't leave her even when they reached Judy's cabin. In fact, it only made it worse as Debbie realized that the door was wide open.

"Someone's inside. Stay here. And call the cops if I don't come back out after 5 minutes." Ed ordered but Debbie was reluctant to agree.

Debbie said, "It's better for us to go together. If he's alone, at least there's the two of us to fight him off."

Ed shook his head. "What's the advantage of two bodies when faced with a cold gun? It'll only endanger us both."

"But we just got back together. I can't lose you now, Ed," she pleaded. The man assured her with a quick kiss and a promise of returning safe before exiting the car. Debbie watched with a heavily anxious heart as her husband entered the suspicious cabin. A minute went on in complete silence, and another and another yet Debbie felt squeamish in her seat. She was ready to bolt out and save Ed in a heartbeat. After the 4-minute mark with still no sign of her husband, Debbie left the car.

She sucked in a deep breath, phone in hand. The woman weighed the consequences of going inside without back-up. Ed would surely be disappointed if she recklessly entered the cabin with nothing to protect herself. She brought nothing with her, no pepper spray or her metal comb. Her car had nothing in it for self-defense. She had nothing but a phone and her bare fists. As she concentrated on what to do, she failed to realize that someone was creeping closer until a hand spun her around. Debbie couldn't even scream in shock, frozen with her eyes wide as saucers.

"You shouldn't be here. Danger. Shh." Bobo whispered, pointing at the open-door cabin. "Killer. Inside. My rat friend and I saw."

Killer... There's a killer inside...

"Ed." She gasped out, pushing Bobo's hand away from hers as she ran inside out of instinct. The blonde didn't even notice that she had let go of the phone in her rush but was immediately jerked back by a horrified Bobo.

"No. No. You shouldn't! The people on the trees knew you were coming," he insisted before tapping on one of his ears. "Listening. They're listening. They knew."

"But my husband-"

Debbie was surprised when Bobo took out an old revolver and handed it to the woman.

Bobo said, "Take this. This makes them go away. Two bullets."

The blonde shakily accepted the gun, gulping as her fingers coiled into the cold metal. It was terrifying to hold a gun, but she braved it for the sake of Ed's safety.

"Thank you. And I'm sorry for accusing you." She said, as the homeless man only nodded. Now armed, she entered the cabin as silently as she could. It was dark, much darker than she expected with the only source of light being the ajar door behind her. She couldn't even see where she was going which was baffling since it was bright outside.

The killer must've blocked every window. She thought to herself as she held the gun tighter.

Then came the rustling. Left, right, darting from the back and to the front. Debbie spun around, trying to detect which way the noise was coming from, completely losing sense of her direction as she turned in circles with her hand held out.

"Alas, the main character appears to save the day." A man's voice rung around the dark cabin. "Came for your poor husband, I assume?"

"Show yourself!" She shouted back, trembling hands worsening by the second. The man laughed at her fear, taunting her even more by walking around.

"Are you afraid, Debbie? You can run back. Go and leave your husband like he did to you." He hissed.

"He kept secrets that put you in this situation when you could've lived a normal life."

"Where's my husband?! What did you do to him!?"

"Oh, I have done nothing yet. Why? Do you want to witness your husband being in pain?"

"Don't you dare."

"Don't I dare?" He scoffed, amused. "Don't you hate him? I know you do. You don't have to lie."

"Shut up! Stop being a coward and face me, Philip!" She screamed, and, as if on cue, a single light bulb flickered, revealing Philip seated next to Ed who was bound on both legs and arms, rope tied around him and a wooden post, lips sealed with a duct tape. Ed's eyes showed fear, not for himself but for Debbie like he was telling her to run away. Debbie pointed a gun at Philip who didn't even flinch. Instead, he showed her at least 15 identical brown-colored keys on a keyring. The blonde also noticed a deep thick glass box container with its half filled with clear water near him when he hovered the keyring above it, though she was certain it was anything but ordinary water.

"I propose a game, Debbie." Philip started, smiling evilly before pointing at a closed door with his free hand. "Behind that door is a friend you know very well. But that's not all. I gave her a little gift."

"What do you mean?" Debbie asked, growing more and more distressed of the situation.

"To put it simply, in 3 minutes, that room will be filled with a highly poisonous gas called hydrogen sulfide. If you find the right key out of these fifteen in here, you can save her. But if not, then she'll be sleeping forever."

"You're not giving the keys with nothing in return."

Philip grinned as if he was almost proud that the woman deducted that much. "How observant! You're correct. This lovely box right here is made of borosilicate glass, the type of glass poor little Judy and cowardly Herman used to work with in the lab."

She didn't like it when the man's grin turned almost ear-splitting as he continued his monologue. "Do you know what's inside this wonderful container? Here, let me give you an example."

The blonde woman stood in utter hysteria as the man dropped a solid penny on the container, bubbling with green swirls mixing with the clear substance before dissolving completely.

"Amazing, isn't it? Concentrated Nitric Acid can dissolve copper rather effectively. It can also synthesize a vast array of other explosive materials like TNT which will definitely be useful for a war. Judy and Herman had quite an intelligent mind to study them. A shame they chose to breach our agreement," he spoke nonchalantly, shaking the keys. "I'm sure you know what these keys are made of now."

"How can you be this evil?" Debbie spoke in disbelief while Philip just chuckled.

Philip replied. "I'm not that evil now, am I? I'm giving you a choice. Kill me, and I'll drop these keys or drop the gun and I'll let you save your dear friend. I'm giving you 3 seconds. The choice is yours, Ms. Heroine. Three... Two... On-"

The sound of metal dropping on the wooden floor was heard. Soon after, an entertained laughter.

"Kick the gun away now, Debbie. We don't want any foul play."

Debbie glared, kicking the gun far from her as Philip snickered. "Very good. Very good indeed."

"Keep your promise. Give me the keys." She demanded. The man tossed the keys towards her as she immediately sorted through the keys, cursing every time the door knob remained lock. Debbie then heard rustling and a soft moan inside, as if someone had finally woken up.

"Hello?! Hello, can you hear me!?" Debbie pounded on the door. "Shoot. Why won't this lock budge?!"

"Debbie? Is that you? Wait... Where am I? Debbie why is the door locked!?"

The blonde's blood ran cold as she heard how scared her friend sounded on the other side, moving so fast to find the rest of the keys that she almost dropped them in a hurry.

"Patty! Calm down, okay? You hear me? I'm going to get you out of there. Cover your mouth with fabric and try not to inhale too much!"

"Having a hard time there, Debbie?" Philip chuckled. In her fury, she charged at him, grabbing a fistful of his collar while demanding for him to tell her which key to use.

"That wasn't in one of my conditions, sorry. But I'm sure you know more than to waste your time with me when you could be helping your beloved friend," he calmly responded. Defeated and clearly distraught, Debbie pushed him away and tried the keys again, crying while apologizing to Patty. The woman's heart broke as she heard her friend's plea and cries gradually growing weaker until she could hear nothing anymore.

Debbie sobbed then and there, her heart breaking with every pound of the door. She had failed Judy, accused

Herman and Bobo and now, she had failed Patty too. She was on her knees in front of the door, her whole body shaking uncontrollably. Her hope of every living a normal life was shattered.

"Ah. So, it seems that not all heroes can save lives. Poor thing."

"What do you want?" Debbie sobbed, already giving up. Philip crouched down next to her, enjoying the despair she was in.

"You know what I want. I want the papers or you can say goodbye to your husband as well." He whispered. The blonde raised her head, dazed as if looking past the man before directing her gaze at him dead in the eyes and answering, **"Go to hell."**

Debbie immediately backed off as Ed, now free from being tied, tackled the man with a rope. She watched as they wrestled before she saw the gun Bobo had given her. Acting quickly, she grabbed the gun and screamed.

"Don't move or I'll shoot!" The two men looked at her and how she was pointing the gun, shakily, at Philip. Ed responded by moving away as Debbie walked closer to the other man, the muzzle of the gun placed directly at his forehead.

"It's over now, Philip. You're going to rot in jail for the rest of your miserable life." Debbie announced, heaving. She expected for him to beg for his life but that never occurred. On the contrary, he was laughing like she had said the best punchline of the decade.

"He's insane." Ed said, looking at Philip with great disgust.

"Oh, but I'm perfectly sane. It's just that I find it funny how you think you've already won the game, Debbie."

"What?"

"Don't believe him, Debbie. He's just playing with your mind." Ed interjected but Debbie felt compelled to hear his words.

"You're too trusting, Ms. Heroine. That has always been your weakness." Philip spoke before the sound of a gun cocking back behind her.

"Put the gun down and raise both your hands in the air, Debbie." A voice said as the blonde slowly obliged, appalled by the first-class seat she was given of seeing Philip's sadistic smirk face to face.

"See? I told you time and time again. You shouldn't have messed with me." Philip told her, moving to pick her gun up. **"You'll never win against me. Not in this lifetime."**

"How can you do this to me?" Debbie whispered to the person behind her.

"I don't have a choice. You decided to get too involved with this case. I tried to warn you."

Philip sarcastically snickered. "Didn't you know? No matter how many times you warn a stubborn person, they'll always be persistent. Why don't we let you in on a little secret now that you are near death's door? Tell it to her face how you killed Judy and Herman."

The person behind Debbie slowly moved in front of her, gun still pointed at the blonde. Disbelief, betrayal, disappointment clouded Debbie's eyes as she came faced the killer she's been looking for, the killer who's been next to her all along.

"You killed them?" she asked, tearing up.

"Please understand. They offered me money, and I badly needed some. I know you understand me."

"I don't! How could you play with my feelings?! How could you act so innocent with me? You betrayed me! I trusted you! **HOW COULD YOU, *PATTY*?!**"

Patty bit her lips, looking away in guilt for a moment before looking back, all traces of humanity gone from her eyes. "Give us the papers, and no one will get hurt. Don't make this too complicated, Debbie. I don't want to hurt you."

"Don't you dare call me by my name. I don't know you anymore."

A gun shot echoed, then an excruciating scream.

"Ed! Oh my God!" Debbie shouted in panic as Philip shot him on the thigh, causing her husband to stumbled down in pain.

"Stop wasting time. We don't have all day." The man clicked his tongue. "Give us the papers."

"Don't! Run away, Debbie!" Ed cried out to her, but she remained in her place.

"Just hand it over, Debbie. Please." Patty whispered. Debbie closed her eyes, swallowing a lump in her throat before reaching her decision.

In a blur, Debbie pounced at Patty who was unprepared, wrestling for the gun as it fired into the roof. The two women were screaming at each other to let go, but not one did. Philip, who was growing irritable, fired another gun towards them, grazing Patty who yelped in pain. The blonde saw that opportunity to steal the gun and aim it at Philip. She wasted no time and pulled the trigger, surprised to learn that it didn't have any bullets at all.

"Ha! You think I'm taking a risk, giving her a loaded gun?! I know she might stab me in the back like those cowards did!" The man laughed psychotically, pointing his gun back at her face.

"Touché, stupid idiot!" Debbie yelled as she attacked Philip next, intuitively using the hard gun to hit his annoying face. Repeatedly. She screeched in agony when the man punched her stomach, curling into a ball as she held it.

Philip stood up, unbalanced and appearing to be furious. Towering over Debbie, he leaned down to choke her.

"Die, you fool!" he spat out. She went into hysterics as he watched her struggle for air, clawing at his arms with blunt nails.

"Let-go… of me…" Debbie choked, gasping hard and almost seeing white swirling around her. She was losing consciousness when the sound of the police siren reached her ears.

Philip cursed, rushing to escape but Ed had another plan as he pushed him with all his remaining strength towards the glass container. Debbie continuously gasped for air while the sound of Philip's scream and the police raiding the cabin resounded around her.

"Debbie… Debbie… Help's here. We're safe." Ed whispered as the surrounding commotion continued. Patty was crying, saying that she was just forced to do what she did, as she was arrested by the police. Philip went limp, his head in the container.

"Don't look. Keep your eyes close until we are out of here." She heard her husband say. The retching noises were enough for her to believe him as they were ushered out by the medical team. Debbie was sure she had some fractured ribs, a broken leg and a swollen face while being carried by a stretcher but she was more worried about her husband who still had a bullet stuck in his thigh at the next stretcher beside hers. Outside, she saw more officers and two ambulances. She also saw the head of the police talking with Bobo who had her phone in his hand.

So, it was Bobo who called the police... Thank God.

Seeing her, Bobo waved and ran. "Your phone. I called them and said the killers were inside. You're okay now. My mouse friend helped you."

Debbie thanked his mouse friend with a smile as she took her phone back before the head officer interrogated him again. Feeling a wave of relief rushing through her as her body finally acknowledge the situation. Despite the pain she was feeling physically, she was filled with joy at the thought that it was finally all over.

We're finally safe now. Ed and I.

"Debbie?" She heard Ed say, turning to her husband who was smiling at her.

"Yeah, Ed?"

"Let's renew our vows at Santorini?" the man asked, reaching out a hand for her to hold. With a choked smile, she held his hand.

"Absolutely."